A NOTE TO PARENTS

Disney's First Readers Level 1 books were developed with the beginning reader in mind. They feature large, easy-to-read type, lots of repetition, and simple vocabulary.

One of the most important ways parents can help their child develop a love of reading is by providing an *environment* for reading. Every time you discuss a book, read aloud to your child, or your child observes you reading, you promote the development of early reading skills and habits. Here are some tips to help you use Disney's First Readers Level 1 books with your child:

★ Tell the story about the original Disney film or video. Storytelling is crucial to language development. A young child needs a language *foundation* before reading skills can begin to emerge.

★ Talk about the illustrations in the book. Beginning readers need to use illustrations to gather clues about unknown words or to understand the story.

★ Read aloud to your child. When you read aloud, run your finger smoothly under the text. Do not stop at each word. Enliven the text for your child by using a different voice for each character. In other words, be an actor—and have fun!

★ "Read it again!" Children love hearing stories read again and again. When they begin reading on their own, repetition helps them feel successful. Maintain patience, be encouraging, and expect to read the same books over and over.

★ Play "question and answer." Use the After-Reading Fun activities provided at the end of each book to further enhance your child's learning process.

Remember that early-reading experiences that you share with your child can help him or her to become a confident and successful reader later on!

— Patricia Koppman
Past President
International Reading Association

First published by Disney Press, New York, New York.
This edition published by Scholastic Inc.,
90 Old Sherman Turnpike, Danbury, Connecticut 06816
by arrangement with Disney Licensed Publishing.

SCHOLASTIC and associated logos are trademarks of Scholastic Inc.

ISBN 0-7172-6528-5

Printed in the U.S.A.

DISNEY'S
DINOSAUR
Two of a Kind

by Judy Katschke
Illustrated by Disney storybook artists

Disney's First Readers — Level 1
A Story from Disney's *Dinosaur*

SCHOLASTIC INC.

New York   Toronto   London   Auckland   Sydney
Mexico City   New Delhi   Hong Kong   Buenos Aires

Aladar and Zini were having fun. "Look, Zini!" Aladar said. "I can reach the top of the tree!"

"Me, too!" Zini said.
"Aladar, my friend, we are
so much alike!"

Suri began to giggle. "Oh, Zini," she said. "How c
a dinosaur and a lemur be alike?"

"I'll *show* you!" Zini said.

"Aladar has a tail,"
Zini said. "So do I!"

"Aladar has a
handsome face,"
Zini said. "So do I!"

SPLASH!

"Aladar has lots of friends,"
Zini said. "So do I!"

"Ooof!"

"Aladar has
a big appetite,"
Zini said. "So do I!"

"Yuck."

"Aladar is a funny guy,"
Zini said. "So am I!"

"What do you call a sleeping dinosaur?"

"A dino-snore!"

"You see, Suri?" Zini said. "What does Aladar have that I don't have?"

"Big feet!" said Suri.

"Aladar, my friend," Zini said, "being different is good, too!"

Enhance the reading experience with follow-up questions to help your child develop reading comprehension and increase his/her awareness of words.

Approach this with a sense of play. Make a game of having your child answer the questions. You do not need to ask all the questions at one time. Let these questions be fun discussions rather than a test. If your child doesn't have instant recall, encourage him/her to look back into the book to "research" the answers. You'll be modeling what good readers do and, at the same time, forging a sharing bond with your child.

Two of a Kind

1. What two characters were being compared?

2. What kind of animal is Aladar?

3. What kind of animal is Zini?

4. Name three ways that Aladar and Zini are alike.

5. Name one way that Aladar and Zini are different.

6. Name ways in which you and a sibling or you and a friend are alike and different.

Answers: 1. Aladar and Zini. 2. dinosaur. 3. lemur. 4. possible answers: they both have tails, handsome faces, lots of friends, big appetites, and are funny. 5. Aladar has big feet and Zini doesn't. 6. answers will vary.